THE CAS
TATTLETALE
HEART

THE CASE OF THE
TATTLETALE
HEART

by Elizabeth Levy
illustrated by Ellen Eagle

SIMON & SCHUSTER BOOKS FOR YOUNG READERS
Published by Simon & Schuster
New York • London • Toronto • Sydney • Tokyo • Singapore

SIMON & SCHUSTER BOOKS FOR YOUNG READERS
Simon & Schuster Building, Rockefeller Center
1230 Avenue of the Americas, New York, New York 10020.

SIMON & SCHUSTER BOOKS FOR YOUNG READERS
is a trademark of Simon & Schuster.
Designed by Vicki Kalajian
Manufactured in the United States of America

10   9   8   7   6   5   4   3   2   1
(pbk)   10   9   8   7   6   5   4   3   2   1

Library of Congress Cataloging-in-Publication Data
Levy, Elizabeth.   The case of the tattletale heart.
(A Magic mystery)
SUMMARY: A young detective and her partner, an amateur magician,
solve a Valentine's Day mystery involving a mummy's finger,
a mind-reading act, and a mysterious laughing heart.
[1. Magicians – Fiction.   2. Valentine's Day – Fiction.   3. Mystery
and detective stories.]   I. Eagle, Ellen, ill.   II. Title.
III. Series: Levy, Elizabeth.   Magic mystery.
PZ7.L5827Cau   1990   [Fic] – dc19   89-31268
ISBN 0-671-63657-x   ISBN 0-671-74064-4 (pbk)

Contents

·· 1 ··

Valentine's Day
Is for Saps

When Kate arrived at school one morning, Ms. Sugarman, her teacher, was stapling hearts above the chalkboard. "Valentine's Day!" said Kate. "I love Valentine's Day!"

"Remember the year Kate gave everybody squirting hearts," said Tracy.

"It was the only valentine I got," Max admitted.

Kate smiled at Max. Last year, Max had been just another kid. This year they were partners in the detective business. MYSTERIES SOLVED: NO JOB TOO SMALL, TOO BIG, OR TOO WEIRD read their card. Kate had to be honest. It wasn't much of a business. If it weren't for the jobs Kate got helping Max do magic shows, there might not be any partnership at all.

"I think the squirting hearts were gross," said Jennifer.

"Remember the year before that?" said Alex. "Kate gave us candy hearts, except they were red-hot pepper hearts."

"You've got to keep Valentine's Day lively, right, Ms. Sugarman?" asked Kate. Kate knew that Ms. Sugarman liked puns, so she thought her teacher would also like practical jokes.

"Valentine's Day is for saps," said Alex.

"Smart aleck!" said Kate. "You're the sap."

Ms. Sugarman frowned. "Valentine's Day is too nice to be ruined by bad jokes. It's a day to celebrate friendship and love. You know, Alex was almost right when he said Valentine's Day was for saps."

"I was?" said Alex, sounding surprised.

Ms. Sugarman nodded. "Alex said Valentine's Day is for saps. Well, in the middle of February, when the trees are beginning to wake up, sap rises. It's no accident that the feast of St. Valentine is celebrated in early spring, "whan euery byrd comyth there to cheuse his mate," as the poet Chaucer said.

The whole class snickered at the weird words, but Ms. Sugarman was beaming. Kate had never known Ms. Sugarman to be so bubbly.

"I've invited Mr. Ross and Mr. Marlin to our Valentine's Day party," Ms. Sugarman continued. "Do we have any volunteers to make the box to hold our valentines? I want hearts, and lace, and..."

Max waved his hand in the air, to Kate's surprise. Max used to be so shy he never said anything in class.

"If Max makes the box, he'll probably put a rabbit in it," said Jennifer.

Max whispered something in Kate's ear.

"Ms. Sugarman," said Tracy, "Max and Kate are whispering. We aren't supposed to whisper in class."

"Tracy's right," said Ms. Sugarman.

Little tattletale, thought Kate. She waved her hand in the air. "Please, Ms. Sugarman, let Max and me make the Valentine's Day box," said Kate. "It'll be the best one in the whole school!"

"It'll probably explode," said Alex.

"I want no squirting hearts at this party," warned Ms. Sugarman.

"We promise," said Kate. "It'll be very sweet."

Tracy snorted. "That'll be the day!"

"Since Kate and Max were the first to volunteer, I'll give them the job," said Ms. Sugarman.

Kate grinned. It's okay for Max and me to have secrets, she thought. We're partners! And Max's secret was great. They would give Ms. Sugarman the best Valentine's Day box ever!

·· 2 ··

Curiosity Kills the Kate

Kate tried to cut out a lace heart, but the lace kept shredding. She glanced over at Max. He was much better at this kind of thing than she was. But Max was busy talking to Mr. Ross, the art teacher. In fact, Max and Mr. Ross had been talking together for a long time.

"Max," called Kate. "We've got to finish our box."

"Just a minute," said Max.

Finally Mr. Ross clapped Max on the shoulder, and they shook hands. Max came over to Kate.

"What were you and Mr. Ross talking about?" Kate asked.

"I can't tell you," said Max. "It's a secret."

"You can't have secrets from me, I'm your partner."

Max looked uncomfortable. "It's got nothing to do with you. Now, what did you want?"

"We've got to finish our box," said Kate. She held up her shredded lace heart.

"I've already done the hard part," said Max. "You can finish up the decorations. I've got something more important to do, and it's got to be done by Valentine's Day."

"What is it?" Kate asked.

"I told you, it's a secret." Max went over to a worktable, across the room.

Kate couldn't believe that Max was keeping a secret from *her*, his *partner*. They were supposed to solve mysteries together, not be a mystery to each other.

Finally art period was about over. "Boys and girls," said Mr. Ross. "It's time to put away your projects."

Kate walked over to Max. "Please, let me see what you're doing," she begged.

Max shook his head.

"Is it a Valentine's Day present for me?" Kate asked.

"Don't be silly," said Max. "Absolutely not for you."

Just then Ms. Sugarman popped into the art room. Kate thought she saw Mr. Ross blush. Max put a large sheet of paper over his project and folded his hands over his chest.

6

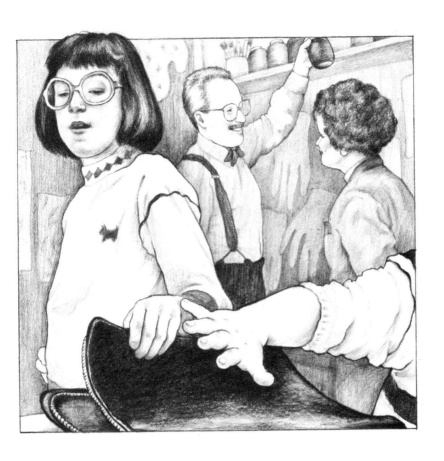

"What's up?" Mr. Ross asked Ms. Sugarman.

Now, Kate thought, it was Ms. Sugarman who blushed. "I...uh...needed to borrow some red paint," she said.

While the teachers were talking, Kate tried to lift the edge of Max's portfolio to get a peek.

Max slammed his portfolio shut.

Kate glared at him. But before she could say anything, Mr. Ross came over.

"Kate, let me see your project," he said.

"Don't you want to look at Max's project?" Kate asked sweetly.

"No," said Mr. Ross. "I'm sure Max has his project well in hand."

Max looked very smug.

"Teacher's pet," hissed Kate.

Mr. Ross frowned as he looked at Kate's lace heart. "Did you plan on making a shredded heart?" he asked.

"Exactly," said Kate. "I wanted something different. I'm sure that in real life every heart is different, like a snowflake."

"That's silly," said Tracy. "Kate doesn't take Valentine's Day seriously enough."

"Ms. Sugarman never should have let *her* make the Valentine's Day box," said Jennifer.

"Why don't you guys find out what Max is making?" asked Kate. "It's supposed to be a big secret!" Maybe she could goad the rest of the class into helping her.

"Can I see, Max?" asked Tracy.

"Yeah," said Alex. "What is it, Max?"

"It's a present for Kate," said Max. He sounded angry. "It was supposed to be a surprise."

Kate was puzzled. Just a few minutes ago, Max had said it wasn't a present for her.

"Is it a Valentine's Day present?" Kate asked.

"It was," said Max. "I was going to give it to you at the party; but since you're so impatient, I'll give it to you now."

Kate felt a little guilty. She shouldn't have tried to pry.

Max took a small box out of his pocket. It looked like a jewelry box. "It's not what you think," he said.

Kate looked at him suspiciously. "What is it?"

"It's something very precious," said Max, "from ancient Egypt. Don't faint."

Slowly Max opened the box for Kate.

Kate pushed aside some of the cotton, and there was a gray-looking finger lying on the cotton.

"It's a mummy's finger," said Max.

"Yuck!" cried Tracy. "That's disgusting!"

Alex was peering over Kate's shoulder, trying to get a better look at the mummy's finger. It had drips of blood around the fingernail.

Suddenly the finger began to wiggle.

"It's alive!" yelled Alex, jumping back.

Kate grabbed Max's wrist. It was his own finger, poked into the box through a hole in the bottom.

"You...you..." sputtered Kate.

Max laughed. "Curiosity kills the Kate," said Max. He took his finger out of the hole and tossed Kate the empty box.

•• 3 ••

Sealed Lips and Magic Tricks

Max worked on his secret art project every day. He wouldn't even give Kate a clue to what it was.

The day before Valentine's Day, Kate lingered at the door outside the art room waiting for Max to finish talking to Mr. Ross. She wanted to bop Max on the nose. She wanted to shake him. Most of all she wanted an explanation. Why was he being so secretive?

Max lifted the sheet from his portfolio and showed something to Mr. Ross.

Suddenly Max saw Kate and pointed to her.

Mr. Ross came to the door. "Kate," he said. "Did you leave something in the art room?"

Kate shook her head. "I'm waiting for Max,"

she said. Behind Mr. Ross, Max growled, "I'm busy."

Mr. Ross closed the door to the art room firmly. Now Kate was really curious.

She put her ear to the frosted glass. She could hear someone laughing, but it didn't sound like either Mr. Ross or Max. Was someone else hiding in the room?

Just then the door opened. Kate practically fell into the art room.

"What *are* you doing?" Mr. Ross said.

"Max wanted me to wait for him," said Kate.

"I did not," said Max.

Kate glared at him. How could he let her down in front of a teacher?

"It's all right, Max," said Mr. Ross. "I think we've done all we can do."

Kate could have sworn she saw Mr. Ross wink at Max.

Max covered up his worktable. "Take good care of this, Mr. Ross," Max said.

As soon as Max stepped into the hall, Kate grabbed his arm. "What's going on?" she demanded.

"I told you," said Max. "It's a secret."

"Valentine's Day is tomorrow. We should be

practicing our act. Instead you're keeping secrets from me!"

For a moment, it looked as if Max felt sorry for Kate. "I'm sworn to secrecy," he said.

"What about being partners?" Kate wailed.

"Kate, trust me," said Max. "This is something I can't tell you."

"Just tell me the truth. Does it have to do with Valentine's Day?"

"You'll have to pull the secret out of me," said Max. He twisted his hand in front of his lips and pretended to throw away the key.

"Your lips are sealed?" Kate asked.

Max shook his head.

"Then you'll tell me?" Kate asked.

Max made a writing gesture with his hand.

"You can't talk, but you can write me your secret," Kate guessed. She took out her notebook and handed it to Max.

"The secret is in my mouth," Max wrote. "Open my lips and pull it out."

Kate looked doubtful. "Is this another trick?" she asked.

Max opened his mouth. Kate saw that he had a piece of paper in it.

She unrolled the paper. Coils of white, orange,

blue, green, purple, and yellow paper came streaming out of Max's mouth like it does in an act in the circus. In fact, Kate knew it was an act. It was paper coils that Max had bought at a magic store. He had played another trick on her!

Now Kate was six feet down the hall, still pulling paper coils from Max's mouth.

Max doubled over laughing. Tracy, Jennifer, and Alex stopped in their tracks. Then they all laughed at Kate, too.

Mr. Ross came out of the art room for his break. He chuckled as he walked down the hall.

Kate picked up the paper lying on the floor and tried to examine it for a secret message. Nothing. It was just a streamer of colored paper.

"Max, have you gone crazy?" Kate asked. This was getting to be too much.

Max just winked at Kate and went down the hall, whistling.

·· 4 ··

The Laughing Heart

The door to the art room was open a crack. Kate looked up and down the hall. It was empty.

Kate debated with herself. On the one hand, Max had a right to privacy. On the other hand, Max was pulling tricks on her to keep her from finding out what was going on in the art room. As Max's partner, didn't she have a right to peek at his portfolio and find out what the big secret was? Kate stopped counting hands. She couldn't help herself. Her curiosity was driving her nuts.

Kate tiptoed into the art room and over to the table where Max had been working. She lifted the cover of Max's portfolio and saw a big heart made out of two sheets of cardboard stapled together and covered with red construction paper. It looked a bit lumpy. So this was Max's secret! Maybe he was planning to play another trick on her at the Valentine's Day party.

Kate's own heart was beating fast. She grabbed the lumpy red heart, and ran out of the room and into the girls' bathroom. At least Max couldn't find her in there.

Just then the bathroom door opened. Kate didn't want anyone to see her with Max's heart. She jumped into one of the stalls and climbed onto the toilet seat so that nobody would know she was in there.

She could hear Jennifer and Tracy giggling. "That was a really neat trick that Max played on Kate," said Jennifer.

"Yeah," said Tracy. "And Kate's always bragging about how they're partners."

Kate bit her tongue. It was one thing for her to be mad at Max, but she hated to have Jennifer and Tracy talking about them. She clutched the heart.

Suddenly, the heart began to laugh.

"What's that!" said Tracy. "Who's laughing at us?" She stuck her head under the door to the stall. "It's Kate!" she said. "She's spying on us!"

"I am not," said Kate, coming out of the stall. "I'm not spying."

"Then why were you laughing your head off?" asked Jennifer. "What was so funny?"

"I don't find anything you do funny," said Kate.

The heart continued to laugh. Kate shook it and it stopped.

"Then why is that heart laughing?" said Tracy.

"It's not mine. It's Max's," Kate blurted out. She could have bitten her tongue.

"That's not funny," said Tracy. "You're going to get in trouble."

"Oh, yeah?" said Kate, holding the heart up

high. "It just so happens I know why this heart is laughing. It's laughing at you two twerps!"

Kate stomped out of the girls' room. She would take the heart right back to the art room, and she'd make Max tell her what was going on.

But when Kate got to the art room, it was locked.

Then, to make matters worse, Kate ran smack into Ms. Sugarman. Quickly Kate hid the heart behind her back.

Ms. Sugarman looked at her watch. "Aren't you due at gym? Don't you have a basketball game this afternoon?"

Suddenly the heart started laughing.

"What's so funny?" asked Ms. Sugarman.

"Nothing!" snapped Kate. "Nothing's funny at all."

·· 5 ··

Double-Faked

Kate hurried down to the gym. She hid the heart in her cubbyhole under her clothes and ran out onto the basketball court. Max was late. Finally he showed up, out of breath. "I have to talk to you," he whispered to Kate.

"I have to talk to you, too!" Kate whispered back.

Just then Mr. Marlin, the gym teacher, blew his whistle.

"We can't talk now," said Kate.

"This is urgent," whispered Max.

Mr. Marlin blew his whistle a second time. "Kate and Max," he called, "are you going to join us?"

Mr. Marlin gave Kate a red vest and Max a blue one. Kate and Max would be playing against each other that afternoon.

Even though they were playing zone defense, Max ended up guarding Kate.

Max waved his hands in Kate's face.

"Out of my way," said Kate as she dribbled in place.

Max waved his hands even harder.

Kate tried to concentrate on the game. She was sure Max would use every trick in the book to distract her. After all, he had been playing tricks on her all week.

Well, thought Kate, Max might be the master magician, but she had a bit of Magic Johnson in her. She dribbled the ball, keeping it well clear of Max.

Max kept up with her moves, even though Kate was the better basketball player. Kate dribbled the ball and faked to the right. She stuck her tongue in the side of her mouth. Kate always did that when she needed to concentrate.

Max realized Kate was faking to the right. He turned to the left. That's when Kate knew she had him. She doubled-faked and went to the right. Kate pivoted and slipped, but even off-balance she made the basket.

"Good basket," Max admitted.

"I faked you out," Kate called over her shoul-

der as she trotted down the court. Now Jennifer had the ball. Kate blocked Jennifer's shot. Kate's team was winning by ten points. Max's team called a timeout.

Alex clapped Kate on the back. "You really faked out ol' Max," he said, admiringly.

Kate nodded. Even though Max was her partner, when they were on different teams, Kate would never want Max to know what she was going to do. She'd always try to fake him out. If Kate could have secrets on the basketball court, couldn't Max have secrets, too?

Kate sighed. Having a partner was complicated. Kate promised herself that as soon as she could, she'd sneak Max's heart back into the art room, and she wouldn't even ask him whom it was for.

Immediately Kate felt better. She made six more baskets in the final ten minutes of the game, making her the high scorer.

Max waited until the crowd around Kate thinned out. "I've got to talk to you," he said.

"Me, too," said Kate.

"Partner," whispered Max, "something terrible's happened. It's a real mystery! I need your help."

"Don't worry," Kate said. "Whatever it is, I can handle it."

They sat down on the bench. "What's the mystery?" Kate asked.

"My project," said Max. "It's been stolen."

Kate swallowed hard. "What project?" she asked, stalling for time.

"My art project," whispered Max. "Kate, you don't know how important it is that I get it back."

Kate swallowed again. Feeling guilty made her mouth very dry. "Uh, how do you know it's missing?" she asked.

"Right before gym I went back to the art room, and it was gone. Mr. Ross helped me look for it. We couldn't find it. He locked the door, but it was already too late."

Kate patted Max on the arm. "Not to worry," she said. "I promise you, you'll get it back."

"When?" asked Max.

"Right after gym," said Kate confidently.

"How can you be so sure?" he asked.

Kate took a deep breath. She did feel bad, but at least she could solve Max's mystery.

"Am I a great detective or what?" Kate asked. "Getting your art project back will be a cinch!"

Max looked relieved. "I knew I could count on you," he said.

Kate didn't have the nerve to tell Max that the reason she could solve the mystery was that she was the culprit. She hoped with all her heart that she'd *never* have to tell Max that.

·· 6 ··

A Last Will and Testament

As soon as gym was over, Kate ran into the locker room. She threw her clothes on a bench and reached into the cubbyhole. She felt around the bottom of the shelf. There was nothing there. The heart was missing!

Kate grabbed her clothes and started to rummage through them.

"You're making a mess," Tracy complained as she put on her jacket.

"Where is it?" Kate demanded.

"Where's what?" said Jennifer innocently. She reached into her own cubbyhole and got her knapsack.

Kate got down on all fours and looked under

her bench. She looked all over the locker room, but the heart wasn't there.

"Kate!" called Tracy. "Max is outside. He's asking for you."

"Tell him I'll be right there," said Kate.

Tracy stuck her head back into the locker room. "Max says that he needs to see you *now*," said Tracy. She had a big grin on her face. "Right now."

Kate knew she had to face the music. She was going to have to tell Max the truth.

Max was pacing back and forth impatiently. When he saw Kate come out of the locker room empty-handed, he lowered his head in despair.

"You don't have it, do you?" Max said.

"Uhh…not at this moment."

"Kate, this is awful," wailed Max. "I've got to get it back."

"It isn't the end of the world," said Kate. "What was so important about that heart?"

"Heart?" Max shouted. "How did you know it was a heart?"

"I…I just guessed. Valentine's Day is tomorrow, you know."

"You didn't just guess." Max pointed an accusing finger at Kate.

Kate looked down at her feet. "I borrowed it," she admitted.

"Borrowed!" sputtered Max.

"We're partners, remember? And you've been playing stupid tricks on me all week. The mummy's finger, the paper streamers—I felt like a fool."

"I was just trying to get you off my scent," said Max. "I didn't want you to be too curious about my project."

"Well, your plan backfired," said Kate. "I was so curious I couldn't stand it anymore. I had to do something."

Max took a deep breath. "Okay, okay," he said. "I won't be mad. Just give it back to me."

Kate sighed.

"Why are you sighing?" Max asked.

"I don't have it…exactly…at least, not at this moment."

"Kate!"

"Well, I'm really sorry, Max. I lost my head."

"I'm going to lose *my* head if we don't get it back."

"Why is it so important?"

"It's for Mr. Ross," said Max. "He trusted me to keep it a secret, and now I've let him down."

"Who was it for?" Kate asked.

"I don't know," said Max. "Mr. Ross had seen one of our magic shows. You know our finale when we pull things out of an empty box?"

"Of course," said Kate. "It's what we're going to do with our Valentine's Day box tomorrow."

"Well, Mr. Ross asked me to help him make a magic heart. He wanted to put some strange things in it."

"What kind of things?" asked Kate.

"Well, Mr. Ross wrote 'Last Will and Testament' on a piece of paper and held it up to a candle so it would look old."

"Maybe he wants to scare somebody."

"I don't think so," said Max.

"What else did he want to put in the heart?"

"A little foam-rubber sheep with a pink ribbon."

"A sheep with a pink ribbon?"

Max shrugged. "That's what Mr. Ross wanted. A Last Will and Testament, a sheep with a pink ribbon, and the letters *E* and *M*. It wasn't so hard to make a magic heart that would hold all those things."

"But why was it laughing?" asked Kate.

"I don't know," Max said. "Mr. Ross put that in

himself. It's a miniature music box from one of those greeting cards that laughs when you open it."

"That's it," said Kate. "Jennifer and Tracy heard it laughing in the girls' room." Suddenly she remembered Tracy's smirking face at the locker room door. Now Kate knew what had happened, but they would have to wait until the next morning to get the heart back. School was over for today.

"What was my heart doing in the girls' room?" wailed Max.

·· 7 ··

Kate the Mastermind

Max and Kate got to school early on Valentine's Day. They waited for Tracy in the playground.

Tracy saw them and made a charge for the door. Max and Kate pursued her down the hall.

"Tracy, come back here," shouted Kate. "You stole Max's heart."

Tracy turned around and smiled smugly. "Oh, Max," she said. "I didn't know you cared."

"Don't be such a jerk," Kate said. "I know you took Max's heart out of my cubbyhole."

To Kate's surprise, Tracy didn't deny it. "You and Max were going to make fun of Valentine's Day," she said. "Ms. Sugarman said we weren't supposed to play jokes this year."

"Give it back!" yelled Kate.

"Tracy," Max wheedled. "Kate might make fun of Valentine's Day, but I never would. Give the heart to me, and I'll make sure Kate doesn't use it to make fun of you."

Tracy crossed her arms over her chest. The look on her face made it clear that she wasn't going to tell them anything.

"Tracy, please," Max pleaded. "You don't realize how important this is."

"How important is it?" Tracy asked.

"It's so important that if you don't tell me, I'll be brokenhearted. My heart might even stop beating," Max said. He winked at Kate. Then Kate knew that Max had a trick up his sleeve.

"Really?" asked Tracy. "It's that important?"

"Absolutely, positively," said Max. He held out his right wrist to Tracy. "Do you feel my pulse?" Max asked.

Tracy nodded.

Max scratched under his right armpit.

"Tracy," said Max in his most serious voice. "If you don't tell me, my heart will stop."

Suddenly Tracy gave a little scream. "Your pulse! It stopped!"

Kate stepped in front of Max. "Tell us where it is," she demanded.

"Ms. Sugarman has it," said Tracy.

"What!" yelled Max, throwing his arms up into

the air. A little rubber ball fell out of his right armpit.

"What's that?" asked Tracy.

"Nothing," said Max, quickly pocketing the ball.

Tracy eyed Max suspiciously. "You don't look like you're dying anymore. Your heart is beating fine!"

"Sorry to disappoint you," muttered Max.

"Why did you give the heart to Ms. Sugarman?" asked Kate.

"Jennifer and I confiscated it," said Tracy. "It was our duty. Ms. Sugarman said no Valentine's Day tricks this year. We figured you were going to make that heart explode or something."

"I'd like to explode you, you little tattletale," said Kate.

"Kate," said Max, "forget about tattletales— we've got to get the heart back."

"Right," said Kate. "Do you have a plan?"

"Me?" Max said. "You're supposed to be the great mastermind."

"Don't worry about a thing," Kate said, a little more confidently than she felt. "I'll come up with something."

"It's now or never," Max said, looking at his watch. "We're running out of time."

·· 8 ··

The Great Mystifying Max

"I've got it," said Kate. "We need a mind-reading act."

"We can't think about adding tricks to our act now," said Max. "There isn't even going to be a Valentine's Day show unless we get that heart back. I'll never be able to face Mr. Ross."

"I mean right now," said Kate. "We need a mind-reading act to get the heart back from Ms. Sugarman."

"Why can't we just tell her it belongs to us. Let's take the simple way out for a change."

"Max," Kate argued, "we've got to be subtle or we'll ruin Mr. Ross's surprise. Now isn't there a mind-reading act where you can make someone come up with the answer you want?"

"Sure," said Max. "It's simple." He explained the trick to Kate.

Kate told Max her plan.

"Maybe," he said, "just maybe."

Together they knocked on Ms. Sugarman's door. It was her free period, and she was putting up the last of her decorations for the party. "Kate, Max," she said with a smile. "Is the box ready?"

"That's why we're here," said Kate. "We're going to do a couple of nice tricks to celebrate Valentine's Day, and we need to practice."

Ms. Sugarman looked doubtful. "Are you sure the tricks are in the right spirit? This particular Valentine's Day is very important to me."

"We just need a teeny-weeny bit of help for our mind-reading act," said Kate. "Can you pretend to be our audience?"

"Well," Ms. Sugarman said. "I do love mind-reading acts."

"Max," said Kate, "get out your magic hat."

Max dug out his collapsing black hat that he always carried in his knapsack. "I'll write down some things around the room," said Kate. "And Max will read your mind. If he guesses right, you have to give him what he guessed."

Kate picked up a pen. She pretended to write down the word "pen." Instead she wrote down "tattletale heart." She said "desk" and wrote down "tattletale heart." She did the same thing for half a dozen other items. Then she folded the papers and put them in the hat.

"Now the Great Mystifying Max will read your mind," said Kate. "Ms. Sugarman, pick out a piece of paper."

Ms. Sugarman reached into the hat. She looked at the slip of paper curiously.

"Don't tell me," said Max. "Just concentrate on the words on the paper. I will draw upon my mystical powers and read your mind."

Ms. Sugarman smiled.

"This isn't supposed to be the funny part," said Kate.

"I see something heart-shaped," said Max. "I see something that Tracy, that little tattletale, brought to you. Eureka!" shouted Max. "I see a tattletale heart!"

Max opened his eyes and looked at Ms. Sugarman.

"Amazing," she said. "That's exactly what's written on the piece of paper I picked."

Kate quickly crumpled up all the other slips of

paper and stuck them in her pocket so that Ms. Sugarman wouldn't find out they all said "tattle-tale heart."

"Now that Max has read your mind, you have to give him the heart. That's the way this trick works."

"Do you mean the heart that Tracy gave me after school yesterday?"

Kate and Max nodded eagerly.

"I don't have it," said Ms. Sugarman.

Kate's mouth dropped open. "Where is it?" she cried.

"Mr. Ross has it," said Ms. Sugarman. "I don't like tattletales, and when Tracy said it was something that Max had been working on in the art room, I figured that's where it belonged. So I took it back there this morning."

"Did you see Mr. Ross?" Max asked.

Ms. Sugarman shook her head. "No, I just left it on his desk," she said.

"Ms. Sugarman, I could kiss you," said Max. "Come on, Kate, we're saved."

"Bye, Ms. Sugarman," said Kate as Max dragged her out the door. "We'll be back in a few minutes to do our Valentine's Day act for the party."

"Bye," said Ms. Sugarman, looking more than a little puzzled.

The great Valentine's Day party was about to begin.

·· 9 ··

Too Great Partners

Kate and Max ran to the art room. Mr. Ross was tying his bow tie. "Max," he said, "it's almost time. Are you ready?"

"Yes," said Max, swallowing hard. He could see the heart on Mr. Ross's desk.

"Thanks for putting this here," said Mr. Ross. "You saved me the trouble of looking for it in your portfolio. I'm glad you found it. You had me worried yesterday."

"Oh, it was nothing," said Max. "Mr. Ross, I hope you don't mind, but I told Kate about it. She's my partner. She helped me get the heart back."

"I don't mind," Mr. Ross said cheerfully. "Just as long as it's back and nothing's missing."

Max checked the heart. "Nothing's missing."

Before Mr. Ross could ask any more questions, Kate and Max got their Valentine's Day box and

41

led him into Ms. Sugarman's classroom. All the kids were in their seats ready for the Valentine's Day party to begin. Mr. Marlin was already there.

Ms. Sugarman smiled when she saw Mr. Ross. Mr. Ross was blushing.

Mr. Ross handed Ms. Sugarman the heart. "Before the party begins, I want to give you this. This is where we met, so this seemed like the place to give you my heart."

Just then the heart began laughing.

"A laughing heart?" asked Ms. Sugarman.

"It's a merry heart," said Mr. Ross. "Open it."

Ms. Sugarman pulled out a yellowed piece of paper.

"What's this?" she asked. "A Last Will and Testament?"

Mr. Ross nodded.

"Keep looking," urged Kate.

Ms. Sugarman pulled out a foam-rubber animal. It had a pink ribbon around its neck.

"A lamb?" she said.

"Look more closely," said Mr. Ross.

"I get it!" said Kate. "It's a girl sheep."

"Who cares if it's a girl sheep or boy sheep?" asked Max.

"Ms. Sugarman, *you* do," said Kate.

42

"A ewe," said Ms. Sugarman, smiling.

"Can you put it all together?" asked Mr. Ross.

"I still don't get it," said Max. "A will...a ewe... a laughing heart."

"A *merry* heart," corrected Kate.

"Will...ewe...merry..." said Max.

Kate clapped her hand over Max's mouth.

Ms. Sugarman pulled out the letter *E* and the letter *M*. "Will ewe merry me?" she repeated softly.

Mr. Ross was blushing.

Ms. Sugarman went over to Mr. Ross. "I have a present for you," she said. She handed him a heart-shaped box.

"Candy?" asked Mr. Ross.

Ms. Sugarman shook her head.

"Why a girl sheep?" Max whispered.

"Because a girl sheep is a ewe, silly," Kate whispered back. "Will ewe merry M E? Let's see what she gave him."

Mr. Ross opened the box. He pulled out a package of artichoke seeds. There was another package of celery seeds.

"Those are the vegetables with a heart in the center, for our garden together."

"She said yes," said Kate happily.

"Boys and girls, and Mr. Marlin," said Ms. Sugarman, "Mr. Ross and I have an announcement. Today, on Valentine's Day, we are officially engaged."

Max still looked a little confused.

"Forget about it, Max," said Kate. "I have a present for you." She handed Max a package.

"What is it?" asked Max.

"Open it," said Kate.

Max saw what looked like an ordinary matchbox, but he knew exactly what it was.

"It has a secret compartment, doesn't it?" he said. Max had been admiring this box for months in a magic tricks catalog.

"You can keep secrets in it," said Kate. "Even from me."

Max grinned. He put the matchbox in his pocket.

"And now, Kate and Max," said Ms. Sugarman, "please bring the Valentine's Day box to the front of the room."

Kate and Max brought out a big box that was decorated with hearts and lace. Max had helped patch Kate's shredding lace hearts and the box looked beautiful.

"This is our Valentine's Day box," said Kate. "As you can see, right now it is empty."

Kate slid the top off the box and tilted the box so that the whole class could see it had nothing in it.

She and Max put the box back on the table and replaced the lid.

"Would the entire class help us by saying 'Abracadabra, Happy Valentine's Day!'" said Max.

"Abracadabra, Happy Valentine's Day," said the class.

Max snapped his fingers. He reached inside and pulled out a beautiful bouquet of paper flowers. He and Kate walked around the room giving everybody a flower.

"I told you it would be sweet," said Kate. She handed the last two roses to Ms. Sugarman and Mr. Ross.

"It's the best Valentine's Day ever," said Ms. Sugarman.

"Now everyone can put their own Valentine's Day cards into the box, and we'll distribute them," said Kate.

Kate wondered if Max had gotten her a card. She had given him a present, but maybe he didn't have anything for her.

Max put his hand back in the box. "Wait a min-

ute," he said. "There's something still in here!"

"What?" Kate asked. She and Max had loaded the box together. There wasn't supposed to be anything in it but the big bouquet of flowers.

Max pulled out a candy box in the shape of a big red heart. He handed it to Kate.

Kate looked at it suspiciously. "Is something going to jump out at me?" she asked.

Max shook his head.

"Can I trust you?" Kate asked.

"It's not a tattletale heart," said Max.

Inside Kate's box were fifteen different-colored candy hearts, each with a different word written on it.

WEIRD was one of them. Then MYSTERIES, HAPPY, JOB, BIG, VALENTINE'S, SOLVED, DAY, TOO, SMALL, PARTNER, NO, TOO, TOO, and OR.

"Too small partners? We're not too small partners," said Kate.

"Put it all together," said Max. Quickly, he rearranged the candy hearts until they read MYSTERIES SOLVED: NO JOB TOO SMALL, TOO BIG, OR TOO WEIRD. HAPPY VALENTINE'S DAY, PARTNER.

"We're too great partners, right, Valentine?" said Max.

"Right, Valentine!" said Kate.

·· 10 ··

How to do
Max's Magic Tricks

The Mummy's Finger

Poke your finger through a hole in a small box
and pack the box with cotton. To make the trick
even spookier, put white makeup on your finger
and paint drops of blood around the fingernail
with red nail polish. When you lift the lid, keep
your finger still and then wiggle it.

The Mouth Coils

Mouth coils are tightly wrapped links of colored paper that can be bought in any magic

store. Or you can make your own (just be sure you use nontoxic tissue paper). Make the paper into links like a Christmas tree decoration, and then carefully fold it into as tiny a package as possible and put in your mouth. Have your partner pull it out slowly.

How to Stop Your Pulse

The trick is to have a ball or a rolled-up handkerchief under your armpit. As you press your arm against your side, the ball stops the blood from going to your hand. CAUTION: Do this for only a few moments at a time.

Mind Reading

The secret of this trick is to write the same thing on all of the slips of paper. It doesn't make any difference which slip is picked. You'll know what is on it because they all say the same thing.

Carefully fold all the pieces of paper so that the writing is on the inside. Ask someone in the audience to pick a piece of paper, read it, and concentrate on the words. Make a big show of working to read his or her mind.

Then when the audience is amazed, casually pick up the other slips and put them out of sight before you begin your next trick.

Your Own Production Box

A production box looks empty, but the magician produces "magic" out of it. Anything can be pulled out of a production box—paper flowers, a rabbit, rubber balls, scarves, candy hearts…anything!

WHAT YOU NEED:

a large cardboard box with a lid
a bag made out of a square cloth with little metal rings at each corner (the color of the cloth should match the inside of the box)
thin black thread
a little hook from a sewing box

BEFOREHAND:

Fasten the hook to the inside of the lid.

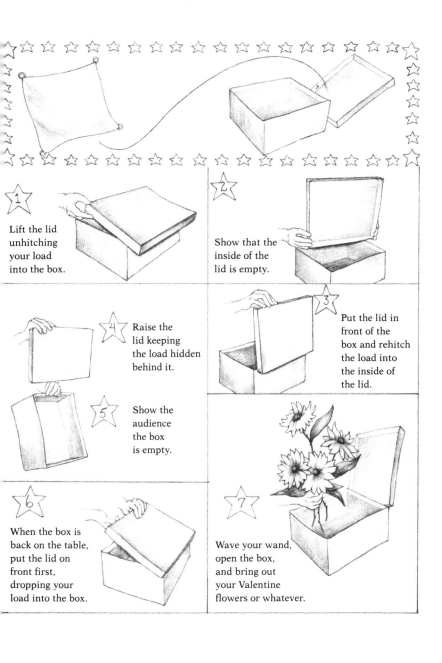

1 Lift the lid unhitching your load into the box.

2 Show that the inside of the lid is empty.

4 Raise the lid keeping the load hidden behind it.

3 Put the lid in front of the box and rehitch the load into the inside of the lid.

5 Show the audience the box is empty.

6 When the box is back on the table, put the lid on front first, dropping your load into the box.

7 Wave your wand, open the box, and bring out your Valentine flowers or whatever.

Put your artificial flowers or anything else you want to "produce" in the square cloth and fasten the four corners to make a bag. Then use extra string to fasten your bag to the hook.

WHAT THE AUDIENCE SEES:

When you lift the lid, you hold the bag behind the lid and show that the box is empty.

Then put the lid on front-first and break the string as you do, allowing the bag to drop into the box.

Say "Abracadabra" or whatever you'd like over the box. Then reach into the box and pull out your surprise.

The Tattletale Heart Rebus

The Tattletale Heart was really just another production box. In this case, Mr. Ross and Max took advantage of the fact that sponge rubber can be held flat between two stiff pieces of cardboard. The ewe was made of sponge rubber. The laughing part of the trick came from a musical card and was flat, as were the "will" and the letters. When pictures stand for words, it is called a rebus.